I Can Read *Comics* introduces children to the world of graphic novel storytelling and encourages visual literacy in emerging readers. Comics inspire reader engagement unlike any other format. They ask readers to infer and answer questions, like:

1. What do I read first? Image or text?
2. Why is this word balloon shaped this way, and that word balloon shaped that way?
3. Why is a character making that facial expression? Are they happy, angry, excited, sad?

From the comics your child reads with you to the first comic they read on their own, there are **I Can Read *Comics*** for every stage of reading:

LEVEL 1	LEVEL 2	LEVEL 3
Simple stories for shared reading.	Engaging stories for children reading on their own.	Complex stories for independent readers.

The magic of graphic novel storytelling lies between the gutters.
Unlock the magic with…

I Can Read *Comics*!

Visit **ICanRead.com** for information on enriching your child's reading experience.

I Can Read *Comics* Cartooning Basics

Panel	Gutter	Tier
A moment in time	The space between panels	One row of panels

Word Balloons When someone talks, thinks, whispers, or screams, their words go in here:

Dialogue · Thought · Whisper · **EXCITED!**

Tails
Point to whoever is talking / thinking / whispering / screaming / etc.

A quick how-to-read comics guide:

In a **panel**, read the text on the **left** first. Then, read the text on the **right**.

On a page, **start here**, in the **top left** corner!

After that, read the panel immediately to the **right**.

When you're done up there, come down here and read **this** panel **next!**

ME NEXT! ME NEXT!

You're almost there...

YOU MADE IT! You just read a comic page!

YAY!

Remember to...

Read the text along with the image, paying close attention to the character's acting, the action, and/or the scene. Every little detail matters!

No dialogue? No problem!

If there is no dialogue within a panel, take the time to read the image. Visual cues are just as important as text, so don't forget about them!

For Taso, who always asked for a story,
and Leo, who always asked for a drawing. —V.F.

HarperAlley is an imprint of HarperCollins Publishers.
I Can Read® and I Can Read Book® are trademarks of HarperCollins Publishers.

Friendbots: Blink and Block Make a Wish
Copyright © 2021 by Vicky Fang

Library of Congress Control Number: 2021933137
ISBN 978-0-06-304945-1 (trade bdg.) — ISBN 978-0-06-304944-4 (pbk.)

Book design by Joe Merkel
21 22 23 24 25 LSCC 10 9 8 7 6 5 4 3 2 1 ❖ First Edition

LEVEL 2

I Can Read!
Comics

FRIENDBOTS

Blink and Block
Make a Wish

by Vicky Fang

HARPER alley

An Imprint of HarperCollinsPublishers

24

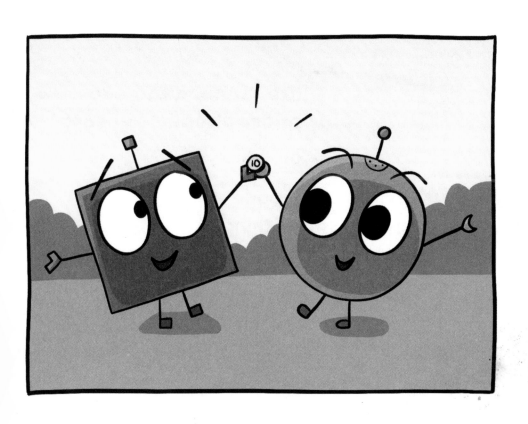

What is a SENSOR?

Robots use **sensors** to understand the world around them.

Like **cameras** to see or **microphones** to hear!

Robots are good at sensing **some** things, but not **everything**.

Yep! Stinky socks? **We don't care!**